Dora's Farm Rescue!

By Christine Ricci
Illustrated by Warner McGee

A Random House PICTUREBACK® Book

Random House 🏠 New York

randomhouse.com/kids
ISBN 978-0-385-38516-9
MANUFACTURED IN CHINA
10 9 8 7 6 5 4 3

One sunny summer afternoon, Dora and Boots were exploring the farm when they heard a noise.

"Uh-oh!" Dora said. "I think I hear someone calling for help."

"Dora! Boots! Help, help! *¡Ayúdenme!*" called Mami Pig.

Dora and Boots dashed over to Mami Pig.

"What's wrong?" Dora asked.

"My three little piggies are missing!" exclaimed Mami Pig. "I can't find them anywhere!"

"Don't worry," Dora said. "We can find those little piggies!" Dora and Boots called for Map, and he popped out of Backpack's pocket.

"I know where you can find the three little piggies," said Map. "In the Big Red Barn! They're stuck! To get to the Big Red Barn, we have to go over the Duck Pond and through the Corn Maze. That's how we'll find the little piggies!"

"First, we need to find the Duck Pond," said Dora.

"I see a lot of ponds, but which one is the Duck Pond?" asked Boots.

"*¡Mira!* There it is!" said Dora.
"Come on! *¡Vámonos!*"

Dora, Boots, and Mami Pig arrived at the Duck Pond. "We need to cross the bridge to get over the Duck Pond," said Dora.

But when Boots tried to open the gate, he found it was locked!

"¡Ay, no!" cried Mami Pig. "We've got to find a way to open this gate."

"It looks like the key to the gate was on this branch," said Dora. "It must have fallen into one of these nests."

"I see it!" squealed Mami Pig. "The key is in the nest with four eggs."

"I can get it!" said Boots proudly. Then he whispered, "Dora? Which one is the nest with four eggs?"

"We can figure it out," said Dora. "Let's count the eggs in each nest."

When they found the nest with four eggs, they counted to be sure. *"¡Uno, dos, tres, cuatro! Four eggs!"*

Boots politely asked the mother duck for the key. Then he passed the key to Dora. Dora unlocked the gate, and the three of them ran across the bridge. "¡Vámonos!" shouted Dora. "Let's go rescue the three little piggies!"

Soon Dora, Boots, and Mami Pig got to a fork in the path.

"Uh-oh," said Mami Pig. "Which way leads to the Corn Maze?"

"Let's think," said Dora. "I can see footprints on each of the paths. We need to figure out which ones are piggy footprints."

"Well," said Mami Pig. "Piggy footprints look like this."

"Over here!" shouted Boots. "These footprints look just like Mami Pig's prints!"

"All right!" cheered Dora. "Let's follow them!"

They arrived at the Corn Maze. "How do we get through, Dora?" asked Boots.

A friendly scarecrow told them, "To get through my maze, you need to take the path that is *amarillo*."

"The yellow path!" Dora said. "Thank you, Mr. Scarecrow! *¡Gracias!*"

Dora, Boots, and Mami Pig looked at the paths. "Here it is!"
said Mami Pig. "This path is *amarillo.*"

"We need to follow that path to get through this maze,"
said Dora.

Dora, Boots, and Mami Pig followed the path out of the Corn Maze.
"We made it to the Big Red Barn!" cheered Dora.
Together they pushed open the barn door. It was very dark inside.
"I can't see anything," said Mami Pig nervously. "How will I find my piggies?"

"Let's see if Backpack has something that can help us see in the dark," said Dora.

Backpack gave them a flashlight. But before Dora could turn it on, they heard a noise. "That sounds like Swiper the Fox," said Dora. "Oh, no!" said Boots. "That sneaky fox will try to swipe our flashlight!" Dora, Boots, and Mami Pig shouted, "Swiper, no swiping!"

Swiper snapped his fingers. "Oh, mannn," he groaned as he ran away.

"We stopped Swiper! Hooray!" everybody cheered.

"Now let's find those piggies," said Dora as she shined the flashlight all around the barn.

"Wow, Dora," said Boots. "Look at everything in here. I can see hay, a wagon, fruit, and vegetables."

"And I see the piggies!" said Dora excitedly.

"We found all three piggies!" said Dora. *"¡Uno, dos, tres!"*

"My piggies!" cried Mami Pig. She was so happy to see her babies. She hugged them and gave them lots of piggy kisses.

"*Gracias,* Dora! Thanks, Boots!" said Mami Pig.

Then the three little piggies gave Dora and Boots juicy red apples to say thank you for helping them.

"What a *farm*-tastic adventure!" said, Dora, giggling. "We did it!"